Bully

The Parent/Student Handbook

VOL. 2

Middle & High School

By Annetta T. Swift

Annetta T. Swift
P.O. Box 1972
Hampton, GA 30228
www.thereadywriter.com
Annetta@thereadywriter.com

ISBN-

Cover Design: Adrian
Graphic and Licensing
PICTURE LOCATION: http://www.officialpsds.com/FIST-THROUGH-THE-WALL-PSD37380.html

Printing by Lulu Press.

Table of Contents

From The Desk of the Author

Greetings Parents, Students and Educators,

It is with great joy and enthusiasm that I pen this book. As a child I was bullied. There were so many times that I wished I had someone to protect and fight for me when I was being assaulted. However, most times I was alone or too scared to tell. As an adult and now a parent, I see things from a different vantage point and now I am determined to make a difference.

It is my goal and desire not only to help and protect the students, but also to assist the educators and parents in bringing this epidemic of bullying to a screeching halt. One person isn't powerful enough to stop bullying, but if enough of us come together, we can make a significant difference in the lives of those are being bullied as well those who bully. "Who is this book written for and who will it help?" may be your questions. The answer is simple. This book is written to ease the mind of parents, give solutions and protection to the students, and to shine light on the bully in an effort to steer them in the right direction.

Do I have all of the answers? No! However, at the end of the day everyone that reads this book will be made aware of the problems and pointed to possible solutions to end bullying.

Sincerely,

Annetta T. Swift

Introduction

There are several types of bullying such as, but not limited to, verbal, physical, and social. However, I would like to hone in on one in particular which is Cyberbullying. First, let's discuss what Cyberbullying means. The internet defines Cyberbullying as using technology to harass, threaten, hurt or insult a person.

Technology is increasing each day, it is virtually impossible to communicate without it. It has made it easy to bully in a plethora of outlets such as: Facebook, Instagram, cell phones, computer and the list can go on for days. Our schools are filled with bullying and Cyberbullying has far surpassed the level of the "typical" bullying. Once a picture hits the internet, it is out there forever. All other bullying can be traced or pointed out by the victim, but not Cyberbullying.

On the contrary, Cyberbullying source can not be traced or deleted. Posts made on the internet can go viral in a matter of minutes and can cause severe damage to a child's self-esteem. This monster Cyberbullying is no longer confined to the school yard, classroom or bus, but it has snuck its way into the comfort of the home.

We will talk more about Cyberbullying in a later chapter, but each person needs to know that Cyberbullying is on the uprise and we must be prepared and aware to make sure that we are not eaten up by this harmful beast.

Bully Me Not

The Parent/Student Handbook

VOL. 2

Middle School

By Annetta T. Swift

Middle School

CHAPTER ONE

"Double Trouble"

People talk about sibling rivalry all of the time, but rarely do they tell of the harsh accounts that happened within the home. My twin sister Traci and I were one account. She was a terror to say the least. It's hard to say if she hated me or if there was something else going on in her head.

The night when everything was exposed is one that will remain fresh in my mind forever. I can still smell the odor in the hospital as they rolled me down the hall faster than a racecar. The paramedic's voices were like echoes, but I could hear what they said clearly. I was in and out of consciousness and the panic in the doctor's voice reassured me that I was knocking at death's door. I could hear my sister crying out to them.

"Don't let my sister die! Please! Laci, I love you! I am sorry for everything!" She screamed as they took me through the double doors.

"I am sorry ma'am, no one can go beyond this point. You can wait in the waiting area and someone will update you. We will do our best to take care of your sister," one of the hospital staff said to her. She fell to the ground and cried uncontrollably.

The events that led up to that moment started years ago. Though Traci and I were twins, we didn't' look alike. We were fraternal twins. She was the "pretty" one and I was not. Our parents never compared us or said any differently. However, in the eyes of the public, she was clearly the prettier twin.

It is often said that twins were close and could feel the other's pain. That was not our case. In fact, Traci was the one who often caused my pain. It was that way since we were small children. It started to become more noticeable and evident to others when we went to middle school. Everything was new for us. We left Chicago to go to Atlanta, Georgia. Our father landed a big job there with Apple.

I looked forward to the change and an opportunity to meet some new friends. We were settled in right at the time the school year began. I was nervous, but I was excited about the endless possibilities that I would have. The school we attended wore uniforms and that was the best thing to me. Traci on the other hand hated it. She was not only pretty, but also enjoyed wearing the latest fashions.

"Look Ug-Moe, don't go around telling people that I am your twin!" Traci scolded as she applied lip gloss in the mirror. I sat at the edge of the bed swinging my legs adoring her as I always had.

"Why not? Everybody will know." I rebutted.

"No they will not. You will...never mind just DON'T say the word twins." She said walking up to me.

"Okay, I won't!" I said looking away from her like a scared puppy. She stood there silently for a few seconds then went back over to the mirror. "Looks like we will all be twins with these cute uniforms." I said admiring my clothes.

"You are so freaking lame. How can you be related to me? Who likes a uniform? I have my own style. This is hideous!" She stopped talking and sneered at me while I admired my image in the mirror. "No matter what outfit you put on you are still dog ugly." She said laughing. The more I starred at her the harder she laughed. Tears filled my eyes because I was hurt and my sister that I loved with all my heart seemed to hate me with all of her's, yet I didn't know why.

"How can you be so mean to me?" I asked crying.

"How can you be so ugly?" She asked still laughing. Our mother came in and as always, I hid my face. Mother was never the wiser. She and Dad were always rushing and on the go. They were movers and shakers, but not the best parents. Though they made sure we had everything, I would have rather had their time and protection from my sister "Cruella".

"Look at my babies! Y'all look amazing in your uniforms!" She cheerfully stated. I wiped my eyes as quickly as I could. I didn't want to deal with Traci's wrath if she got into trouble with Mother. I learned early on how to act like everything was perfect with us. "You guys make sure you stick together and look out for each other. Middle school is different from when I was a little girl."

"Yeah like a million years ago." Traci said laughing.

"It wasn't that long ago, but the way technology is, you would think that it was that long ago." She turned to me. "Are you ok, Laci?"

"Yes, Mother. I am just nervous, that's all." I said. I was relieved that she didn't notice that I had been crying. Traci came over and hugged me. My beautiful sissy and I are going to have a great first day, isn't that right? We were just talking about how we have to stick together." She said winking at me. I was speechless at first. Before I could answer, Mother had already grabbed us for a group hug. Traci looked at me and rolled her eyes. I felt like I was in a movie. Better yet a nightmare that I was not about to wake up from.

Surprisingly we didn't have any of the same classes. This made Traci happy and surely made things easier on my end. I made sure to avoid her at all cost. We were in eighth grade which was almost like being a senior in high school only for middle school.

I got lost trying to find my classes all day. Traci undoubtedly had already made friends. I saw her after my lunch hour. She was with two other pretty girls. I wanted to say hi at least, but when she spotted me she turned her head. The most embarrassing part of the day was when I went into the wrong classroom. When I walked in all eyes were on me. I hurried and sat at a desk.

"What is the funny looking chick doing in here?" Traci asked aloud. My heart sank. I knew then that I was in the wrong place, but I was too afraid of what she would say if I got up. The students in her area were laughing like she was a comedian. I am not sure of what she was saying about me, but it gave me the courage to get up and leave out. I raised my hand and told the teacher about me being in the wrong class. I showed her my schedule and she led me in the right direction.

As I walked toward my correct class there was another girl heading the same way.

"Hey girl!" She said as if we knew each other.

"Hello…," I said looking at her strangely.

"What class are you late for?" She asked.

"How did you know I was late?"

"I am late and there is no one else in the hallway…" She looked around the hall. "Yeah, so I figured that was the case. My name is Aubrey and you are?" She asked extending her hand to shake mine. She was texting with the other hand. She was pretty and friendly. As fate would have it, we were going to the same class which was comforting to me. Aubrey ended up being my new best friend. We did everything together until she had cheerleading practice.

As the school year passed, Traci and I hardly ever crossed paths. She was only mean to me at home. We rarely every physically fought. But one day I had enough of my sister's cruelty toward me.

"Ok, Laci, my mom is going to pick you up tonight at 6:30 p.m. make sure that you are ready." Aubrey said via text.

"Kk..." I replied. I was extremely nervous. One of her cheerleading friends was having her birthday party at the skating rink. I didn't feel like I fit in being the "Ugly Duckling", but Aubrey acted as if I was as pretty as she was.

Once we arrived and got our skates, Aubrey took me over to meet the birthday girl and her "crew". When we got to where they were, there was Traci standing in the middle of their group. I took a deep breath. Once she noticed me she had a fit.

"No! What is she doing here?" Traci asked one of the girls. She had the biggest frown on her face. My heart sank once again. It was one thing for her to be mean at home, but she had rarely humiliated me publically. My heart started beating fast and my breaths became shorter.

"Are you ok?" Aubrey asked me.

"Yeah, Yeah, I'm ok." I said.

"Hey Guys!" Aubrey shouted. They returned the excitement with random, "Hey girl..." They each hugged and then there was the introduction.

"This is my best friend that I was telling you about Ke'andra." Ke'andra waved at me happily. "Everybody this is Laci and Laci this is everybody." She said smiling as if she was presenting a superstar.

"Hey Laci," they all said in unison.

"Hey!" I said shyly. I was watching Traci who didn't open her mouth to say a word to me.

"I'm leaving. This chick here is wrecking my flow. I cannot do this..." Traci said taking off her skates.

"Why are you tripping?" Aubrey said.

"It's this thing right here." She said pointing at me. I looked down at the floor.

"Wait, y'all beefin'?" Aubrey asked. Aubrey looked at Traci who didn't respond and then she looked at me. "Hello? What's going on?"

"Aubrey, Traci is my sister." I said.

"Now, I am really confused." Aubrey said.

"I am NOT your sister. We are related but not blood related. She lives with us. Nothing ugly like that thing could be related to me." Traci said.

At that moment it was as if she had stabbed me in my heart. Some of the girls were laughing and agreeing with her. For years I was her target and I wouldn't stand up for myself much.

"Hold up! This is not how we get down. We may not all get along, but we don't put anyone down like that in our group – especially family!" Aubrey said looking at Traci.

"Look, you don't know me like that so fall back. This ain't what you want." Traci said walking up to Aubrey.

"Girl, you better get out of my face." Aubrey said looking her in the eyes.

"I will just wait outside. I am not trying to mess up this birthday party. I'm sorry." I said as I walked away crying.

"Don't go!" Aubrey said as I walked toward the restroom. I entered the restroom and Traci entered after me. Something in me felt as if she would be remorseful for what she had done to me.

"I told you not to tell anyone that I was your sister!" Traci shouted.

"I am not ashamed of being your sister. I am proud..." Traci slapped me in the face. There were already a few people in the restroom. I shook myself and before I knew it we were fighting. I don't know who got the best of whom. I just know that the person that I loved dearly had crossed the line and my heart was broken. I called my mother to come get me. I didn't tell her about the fight. I just told her that I had vomited. As usual, she was too busy. She told me to call a cab and where I could find some money in the house.

Once I got home I went into the bathroom and looked at myself in the mirror. My eye was black and there were scratches everywhere - even on my neck. I cried while looking at my reflection. It would have been different if this abuse was coming from a stranger, but my heart could no longer take the agony of knowing that my sister hated me. My twin sister wanted nothing to do with me. It had been that way since we were small children. She was always the smartest one. I was sickly and constantly in the hospital until I turned 11 years old. I didn't want to deal with the possibilities of something worse happening. I went into my mother's room and got some pills out of her drawer. I counted them and went back into my bathroom. I took every pill. That is how I ended up here at the hospital. When Traci came home she found me and call 9-1-1.

We will find out more of Laci's story in a later chapter. Let's chat!

Let's Chat

These questions may be discussed with your parents, teachers and/or classmates.

1. What are your thoughts about Laci and Traci's story?

____

____

____

____

____

2. What makes this bullying story different than any other story?

____

____

____

____

____

3. If you were Aubrey, what advice would you give Laci? Why?

4. What would you do as an onlooker/witness to the fight between the sisters at the Skating Rink?

5. How would you handle the situation if you were Laci? Why?

CHAPTER TWO

"Sweet and Fat"

Being different and a misfit was common place for me. I am not sure if my chromosomes were mixed up or if I was destined to be an outcast. Growing up in a house with all girls made being masculine a hard chore for me. My father was never around and I don't remember ever meeting him. I had a sad a lonely road to travel. Throughout elementary school kids called me gay. My sisters have always called me gay. Even my mother said I was gay. I gathered from what was fed to me that I was gay. I didn't want that title because it was typically frowned upon. My feminine ways came from my example at home.

My first year of middle school went better than I thought. Being gay seemed normal and I wasn't the target of any jokes. However, when I went to 7th grade it was as if I wore a sign saying, "Pick on me I am gay." The thing was I had never had an encounter with a boy or anyone for that matter. Who set the scale or determined if someone was gay? School was scary, but most of my attacks were on my way home. Me and my best friend Dakota were teased a lot. She was on the chunky side and she always got picked on. That was what made us become so close. We were there for each other.

"Look at couple of the year. Fatty and sweetie." Jaylin said laughing with his friends as we passed their house.

"Come on let's walk faster so they won't mess with us." I said picking up my pace. She struggled to keep up with me.

"No, I am tired. We are walking fast already and it's hot." Dakota said. I slowed down to make sure she was ok. We continued to walk and Jaylin and his boys followed us. That was what I was trying to avoid, but it must have been my fate. Once Dakota got to her house I got scared. I didn't want to deal with their slurs, but I had to get home so that I could let my little sister in.

Suddenly, I got a kick in my back that sent me to the ground, face down. As I attempted to get up, Xavier, one of Jaylin's friends, stepped on my back.

"Get off of me!" I said.

"You know you like my foot on your back, punk!" Xavier ranted. "I should just kick your butt to make a man out of you. That is all it will take."

All of them laughed. I tried not to cry, but the blow to my back was so painful and I was afraid.

"Come on y'all let's show Cutie Pie here how to be a man!" Jaylin said helping me up. He punched me in the chest. The hit was so forceful it took my breath away. Two other boys grabbed me and they pulled me back towards Jaylin's house. I kicked and screamed, but no one heard me. Not even Dakota. There were cars riding up and down the street but no one stopped to say anything. I didn't know what they were going to do to me and I knew if I hit one of them, the rest would jump me. The only thing I knew to do was to use the restroom on myself.

"Did this fool just pee on himself? Bruh, come on son!" Jaylin scolded. "You just peed on my momma's couch. Clean it up fool."

"I just want to go home." I said letting the tears escape from my eyes.

"Not only is he a gay punk, he is a pee-pot and a cry baby!" Xavier said. All of them were laughing except for Jaylin who was petrified about his mother getting on him for her urine stained white sofa. "Bruh, ain't no hope for you!" Xavier said.

"Get out my house sissy!" Jaylin said pushing me to the door. I wanted to say something smart, but the prize that I left him said enough. It was the only weapon that I had.

As embarrassed as I was, I was able to find the humor in Jaylin's pay back. I had no idea of what would happen the next day, but I was glad to make it home that day. I called and told Dakota what happened and she was angrier than I was. As usual we sat on the phone and gripped knowing the next day we would say nothing in the faces of our torturers.

"I want to see if we can go a different way home." I said as we ate our lunch.

"My house is a straight shot from here. I can't do that." Dakota said.

"I want to tell the principal." I said.

"No! Do you know what they would do to us then? I don't even want to imagine." She said shaking her head.

"We can't run forever." I stated.

"I may be fat, but I will run as long as I have to. I will catch my breath eventually." Just then Jaylin come over to our table. I sighed.

"I got in trouble because of you." He said. I didn't respond. "You give me a toothache you are so sweet." He turned to Dakota. "And you Miss Piggy give me a belly ache. Y'all were meant for each other."

"Why don't you kick rocks! You are so mean and we are tired of it!" Dakota said. My mouth dropped opened. I knew we would be in for his wrath after that.

"Bruh, you talking to me like that looking like a beach whale."

"Bruh, back to you...I will not say what you look like in the 7th grade again. I rather be fat than dumb any day.

"Dakota!" I shouted.

"I am just saying." She said rolling her eyes eating the rest of her sandwich.

"You got all that mouth in school. But you have to waddle home. I am going to start calling y'all pancake and syrup. You are so round and..." He turned back to me. "Bruh, you are sweeter than sugar. Maybe y'all can get married and raise a bunch of pigs. No, better yet you will be married to a pig. Y'all can make honey baked hams." He said laughing as he left our table and went back to his.

"Why did you say anything?" I asked whispering.

"I am tired of them and if we keep acting scared, they will keep on messing with us." She said.

"No, if we do what you did we will definitely get beat up."

"Look Chance, I don't know what to tell you. I was in survival mode." She said.

"Don't 'look Chance' me! You were in stupid mode and for sure we will have to pay for this." I shook my head and sighed.

"I am not stupid." She pouted.

"I am sorry. You are not stupid. I am scared and I want to tell the teacher or someone."

"The teacher sometimes laugh too. I know one time I fell in the hallway and Jaylin and his friends started screaming, 'Earthquake!' Mr. Johnson helped me up, but he was fighting back his laughter."

"There has to be someone who we can tell."

"Chance, there are plenty of people we can tell. There just isn't anyone that will keep them from bothering us again. Bullying is everywhere. Don't nobody really care. We just have to get through it the best way that we can." What she said was true from what I had experienced. As bad as I wanted to tell someone, I wanted not to get beat up more.

On our way home Dakota insisted that we stopped by her house to come up with a solution. When we go inside the house her aunt was cooking dinner. The aroma was strong enough to make you feel like you could taste the food. I followed her into the basement after we "stalked" her aunt in the kitchen. She went over to a closet and pulled out a small safe.

"What is that?" I asked

"It is our answer." The safe didn't have a lock on it. She opened it and pulled out a gun.

"No! No! NO! Dakota, No!" I yelled.

"Shut up! You are too loud." She said with an evil grin.

"If we take this to school we will be expelled for good!" I said.

"Who said anything about taking it to school? You take it home with you and if they come messing with you, shoot 'em." She said. "Well, not for real. There are no bullets in here see." She pointed the gun at me playfully.

"Girl, stop, don't play with guns!" I scolded trying to grab it from her. We tussled and wrestled until the "empty gun" fired. We both screamed and her aunt ran downstairs where we were. I was shaking like a leaf and so was Dakota. There was so much blood that I didn't know whether I got hit or her...

We will find out what happened with Chance and Dakota in another chapter. For now, let's chat!

Let's Chat

These questions may be discussed with your parents, teachers and/or classmates.

1. What are your thoughts about Chance and Dakota's story?

____

____

____

____

____

____

2. What makes this bullying story different than any other story?

____

____

____

3. If you were with either Chance or Dakota what advice would you give them? Why?

4. What would you do as an onlooker/witness to the beating that Jaylin and his friends put on Chance?

5. How would you handle the situation if you were Chance or Dakota?

____

____

____

____

____

6. Would you tell anyone? Who would you and why?

____

____

____

____

____

High School

CHAPTER THREE

"Stand By Your Man"

My best friend Alundra and I sat in the principal's office waiting for him to enter and give us the punishment that fit our crime. If anyone would have told me that the girl that I grew up with, who was more like my sister, would end up my enemy I would not have believed them. I sat across from her with my legs crossed dangling from side to side. She was looking in the mirror at the plethora of scratches on her face. I wasn't a fighter, but I was pushed into a corner and I came out swinging. The principal came into the office shaking his head.

"Ladies, I am disappointed to say the least. You two are some of the best students here. I can't believe that you are in my office for fighting each other. I thought you were best friends." He said looking at both of us. Neither of us said a word. "Well, don't all speak at once." He said sitting at his desk."

"I didn't want to fight her. She started it. I thought she was my best friend." I said looking at her.

"I thought you were mine, until you..." Alundra stated rolling her neck.

"Okay Ladies. One at a time. Let's start with you Minyom. What happened?" He said as he rested back into his chair.

"It's a long story." I said.

"Give me the shortest version that you have, Minyom." He said chuckling.

"I took chorus and met this guy named Omar. He plays football and he loves to sing." I said.

"I know Omar." Mr. Johnson said nodding his head.

"Anyway, I didn't know that Alundra liked him or dated him."

"Yes you did. Just tell the truth! You ain't nothing but a freak!" Alundra yelled.

"I will hear your side, let her speak now." Mr. Johnson chided.

"I did know that Alundra had a boyfriend. We tell each other everything, but I swear she never mentioned Omar's name. She kept him a secret. She had some kind of nick name for him. I never met him and we started dating. He told me he had just broken up with his girlfriend and as far as I knew she was still with her bae. Once she found out that Omar was the guy she dated she flipped out on me."

"I am about to flip out on you again." She said scooting to the edge of her seat.

"Pick your mirror back up and you will see who flipped out on who. Don't come for me. I don't care who is in here." I said.

"You don't?" Mr. Johnson asked.

"I'm just saying. No, disrespect, Mr. Johnson." I said continuing my story. Once we were done explaining both of our sides, we ended up with only three days of suspension. I missed Alundra tremendously. We always talked and hung together, but it seemed that Omar drove a wedge between us.

I was on punishment and I only had access to the internet during the times when my mother was home. She took my cell phone and I was miserable. I felt bad for fighting Alundra, but she kept calling me out of my name. She was also spreading rumors about me and Omar sleeping together. I was still a virgin and vowed to be one until I got married. I would have never dated him if I had know before we got involved. I didn't think I had to break up with him to salvage our relationship because if tables were reversed, I wouldn't have been angry with her. I didn't purposely go after him and they were no longer together.

The second day of my punishment and suspension my mother gave me back my phone. She understood as well, but I had to use it after six in the evening. During the day I had to do my work and chores around the house. I was like an addict. I went straight to Kik and Instagram. Surprisingly the first thing that I saw was a picture where someone pasted my picture on the body of a prostitute. I was floored. There were several pictures of me floating around as a joke and it went viral. People were sharing this and calling me a whore all over social media. My reputation was being smeared while I had never done more than kiss a boy. I called Alundra right away. She answered rudely.

"What do you want female?" She said laughing.

"Why did you do that?" I asked.

"Do what?"

"Alundra, don't play stupid! You know what you did with my picture. It is all over social media. People that don't even know are sharing the picture that you created of me." I said.

"First of all, don't call my house with your crazy accusations. Secondly, I didn't make a picture of you!" She said and ended the call. I was enraged. I went to look at Facebook and there were other pictures of me surfacing. All in one day. I sent Omar a text.

"Hey bae"

"Hey what's up" He replied.

"IMU!" I texted.

"IMU2" He replied.

"Did u kno about the pics of me?"

"Wat pics?"

"memes of me r on IG, Kik, FB evrywer..."

"Oh yeah that..."

"wat u mean that?????"

"I did c it"

"Did u share it or laff?"

"Share no. Laff 1 time."

"r u kiddin me?"

"Yeah, I didn't laff but I do hav somp 2 tel u..."

"Wat????"

"We can't go 2gethr no more?"

"wat? Y?"

"im not feelin this no mor srry..."

"Plz tell me y? wat did I do?" He never replied again. I started getting texts from friends and relatives. By the time a week had passed I put on a cartooned video. My image, which only my face was authentic, was going global with just a push of a button. I cried and didn't even want to go to school. People believed that it was me and that I was the person that social media painted me to be.

There was no way to trace where it started according to some of the staff at the school. My principal said that it would die down just as all other rumors did. This one didn't. I knew within my heart that Alundra was behind it, but she would never admit to it. I had no proof of her crime and no one to defend me. My mother could do nothing because it was too far gone. I was pure as the driven snow, but the internet had me displayed as a degraded female with nothing but boys on my mind. The harassing texts and inboxes were growing by the thousands. I deactivated my accounts, but it didn't stop the videos or pictures from surfacing. I started skipping school in order to avoid the insults and teasing. One day I had enough and went to confront Alundra. When I went to her class Omar was holding her hand while he sat on her desk.

"I guess this is the reason that you let me go?" I said as I approached Omar. The bell hadn't rung yet and there were a few minutes remaining for us to get to our next class.

"I don't know what you're talking about," Omar said kissing her on the hand.

Alundra threw her head back as if she was a queen. I lunged toward her and knocked her out of her seat. Once again we were fighting but this time she got the best of me. The teacher came and broke us up and we ended up back in Mr. Johnson's office again.

We will revisit Alundra's story in a later chapter. For now, let's chat!

Let's Chat

These questions may be discussed with your parents, teachers and/or classmates.

1. What are your thoughts about Minyom and Alundra's story?

____

____

____

____

2. What makes this bullying story different than any other story?

____

____

____

____

3. If you were friends with either Minyom or Alundra what advice would you give them? Why?

4. What would you do as an onlooker/witness to the fight between Minyom and Alundra?

5. What role do you think Omar played in the girls' drama?

6. What is the difference in Cyber Bullying and the other types of bullying? Which is worse?

____

____

____

____

CHAPTER FOUR

"Touch Down"

Football was my life and all that I ever dreamed of doing. I knew that I would one day play pro-ball and my parents did everything to help cultivate my talent and skills. They also made sure that my path was academically sound. That didn't deter me. It only stirred me to press harder toward my goal.

In middle school I became popular for my game, but the girls weren't too fond of me. I had been teased my whole life about the complexion of my skin. Though I was not from Africa the mean things that the children said about how dark I was made me feel that way. It made me feel black, ugly and worthless.

Once I got to high school that changed as my popularity grew. Though my complexion was dark, the girls accepted me as I was. I was known throughout the school system for my ability to play a great game of football. I was good to the point that in my freshman year the coaches allowed me to play on the varsity team. Needless to say, there were varsity players that didn't care for my presence. During my senior year, Blake was my terror. Our school was predominantly Caucasian, but race wasn't a big issue. Blake on the other hand made his disgust for my skin tone a problem. The thing was, Blake was black too. He was light skinned and the girls loved him. It was one thing to deal with prejudices with a different race, but weird for the same race to discriminate against you.

"Yo, man, why don't you quit trying to take so much shine on the field? There is no 'I' in team?" Blake ranted after one of our biggest wins I got for our team.

"What are you talking about, Blake? We won. If I shine, we all shine. It's not about me, it's about the TEAM." I said wrapping my towel around my waste. I had just finished showering.

"You were all up in the cameras and everything! I can't see how they saw your black butt. They probably couldn't see nothing more than your teeth." Blake said.

"I am going to let you slide with that. You're just a little jealous that the girls was all up on me. There are plenty out there for all of us." I said sitting on the bench between the lockers.

"Hey, man, chill out! Why are you sweating my man Logan? He does show out some times, but he is the best thing that has happened for this team and this school. It doesn't take away anything from us. I got mad game and plenty of females. Don't hate, appreciate!" Jevon said giving me dap.

"You still ugly. Wait, why am I calling you ugly? I can't even see your face to ..." I jumped up in Blake's face before he could finish his sentence. Jevon pulled me back.

"Man, this dude ain't even worth messing up all the stuff you got lined up for your future." Jevon said. I nodded in agreement as I stepped back. Jevon grimaced at Blake as we went to the other side of the locker room.

Things went on like that even after football season was over. Though I wasn't the sensitive type, what he said about me got to me. I was adopted and as a little kid I would often wonder if my mother gave me up for adoption because she hated the way that I looked and how dark my skin was. I would be secure around certain people, but Blake and those that boldly talked about my blackness and ugliness made me shutter.

Armani, one of the cheerleaders that I tutored in math was trying to date to me. I didn't want to get involved with her because she was related to Blake. She was his sister. It made things difficult in my head. She was stunning and all the guys wanted to talk to her. No one would because of Blake. He was what most people considered to be the "Tough Guy". He wore the title well, but something in me felt he had some things about himself that he didn't like.

"You are super intelligent, Logan..." Armani said smiling at me.

"I try. Let's get back to this last problem. If X = 6 then..." I stopped talking to look at her as she stared me down. "Armani, you have to pass this test in order to bring your grade up. Looking at me is not going to help." I said sternly.

"I love it! Brains and aggression. I am going to marry you." She said grabbing my hand. I jerked back.

"Stay focused." I said then I heard what she said in my head again. Girl, not in this lifetime. Your crazy brother would have me killed first." I said.

"You won't be marrying him. I would be your wife." She moved back.

Are you telling me you are not interested in me?" She asked standing to modeled for me.

"This is not what we are here for." I said ignoring the beauty that I beheld.

"Okay, I promise not to distract you anymore during this session. Why don't you come over my house and have dinner with us?" She asked. "Then we can finish our math and eat some good food. Well, my mom doesn't cook but she orders and picks up fast food like a beast!" She said laughing.

"Nah...I am good. I need to get home anyway."

"Why? Don't you drive? I need a ride home?"

"Dang girl, you are more than persistent. Ok, I will take you home, but I am not staying if your brother is there." We packed up her books and I drove her home. I wished that I had followed my gut instinct and stuck to my "No".

"We sat, ate and talked for a while. Their mother was equally as beautiful and very charming. It was hard for me to fathom how Blake was such a mean person. He always teased and picked on people with handicaps and of course the physically unappealing. Their mother left to go to work and I used that as my excuse to leave. Armani didn't want me to go, but I left out anyway. She walked me to my car.

"Thank you for the tutoring and thank you for hanging out with me. You are a delight." She said holding my hand. When I went to get into my car, Blake drove up and blocked me in. He got out the car shaking his head.

"Well, well, well! If it isn't Blacky and the Beast." He said laughing.

"Blake, don't start. Just go inside the house." Armani said blocking him from coming to the side that we were standing on.

"I know you ain't liking this dude. Can you see him out here? It's getting dark and he is darker than night. Wait, his teeth are white. Smile for us and bring us a ray of light." The more jokes he made the angrier I became, but I didn't want to fight in front of Armani. I didn't want to fight at all.

"We are too light and pretty for him. He is not your type." He said as he continued cracking on me.

"I don't have a type. He is human and he is sweet. He is a bigger man that you will ever be." She said. That struck a nerve with him and apparently her words stung. He grabbed her by her face and held it tightly.

"Naw, man, get your hands off her!" I said grabbing his arm. He jerked back and punched me in the face. That was the welcome mat that I needed. I proceeded to fight him against what I had previously intended. After a few punches and wrestling in the grass, I got the best of him. I got into my car and left.

The next day at school I knew there would be more drama, but I insisted on not fighting. I was prepared for his insults and I was going to ignore him. To my surprise he didn't say anything to me. After school he and another guy from the team were waiting at my car for me.

"Look man, not today. Just move away from my car and everything will be fine." I said pulling out my keys.

"Everything is already fine." He said. "I see you are not as big and bad as you were last night. My sister ain't around."

"Your sister has nothing to do with this."

"You tried to play hero when I was disciplining her and that is one thing you don't do. Interfere in a man's family life." He said scratching my car with a metal envelope opener.

"Man, my car! What are you doing?" I shouted. Tone, the guy that was with him held me back. I broke a loose from his grip and once again fought Blake. This time we both arrested. I tried to keep my cool and be the nice guy, but luck didn't want to stay on my side.

We will see how this saga ends later in the book. Right now, let's chat!

Let's Chat

These questions may be discussed with your parents, teachers and/or classmates.

1. What are your thoughts about Logan's story?

____

____

____

____

2. What makes this bullying story different than any other story?

____

____

____

____

3. If you were friends with Blake what advice would you give him and why?

____

____

____

____

4. What would you do as an onlooker/witness to the fight between Logan and Blake?

____

____

____

____

5. What role do you think Armani played in this scenario?

____

____

____

____

CHAPTER FIVE

"Anti-Bullying Rally ~ THE SOLUTION"

The city of Atlanta was buzzing with anticipation about their big anti-bullying rally. Schools from districts state wide were in attendance. There were hundreds upon hundreds of people there. The music was playing. Free food and prizes were given. Lives were about to be changed. The auditorium was brightly decorated and the excitement could be felt in the air. Parents, students and educators were all in one place at one time with one goal - TO END BULLYING.

Laci, Chance, Logan, Armani, Darlene, Kaitlin and their parents were there as well. They each went to different schools in the city, but all had a common problem. As everyone was seated the music and the lights were lowered. The news media was there along with journalists and some of the local newspaper staff. The spotlight hit the host of the event, Sannetta Smith. She was an expert on the subject and the reason for everyone being there.

"Good Afternoon Everyone!" Sannetta said with excitement.

"GOOD AFTERNOON!" The audience responded cheering.

"I am your host, Sannetta Smith and I am excited about what we will see and hear today!!!" The crowd roared with cheers and thunderous applause. "We are here to KILL the MONSTER called BULLYING! And we will NOT stop until we slay this giant! ARE YOU WITH ME?" Everyone stood to their feet in agreement. "We have a lot of work to do, but it can be done. As a child I was bullied and I understand the pain and fear that the victims feel. It makes you feel HORRIBLE! I remember being a child and having other children tease me for being chubby. I remember giving up my lunch to keep me from being beaten up. Sometimes I still got bullied and teased even when I gave in. I understand what our children feel. Now I am an adult and a parent and I see it from both perspectives. Guess what? It's scary from all angles.

I have also worked with children and sometimes we miss what is happening up under our noses. So today is dedicated to each of you. When you leave here today you will be empowered and ready to do all that we can to end bullying! " The audience applauded. "I have to be honest. I don't have all of the answers, but I have strategically sought out other bullying advocates as well as done research to see how we, together, can bring bullying to a screeching halt one school at a time. Even if we can't stop it, we can certainly make it hard for this monster of bullying to survive.

I have a special guest with me who is not a victim of bullying, but he used to be a bully. Now he has joined forces with us to help us fight this enemy. The best way to defeat an enemy is to know his strategy and the reason they do what they do. Please make welcome, Mr. Arnold Fredrickson." Everyone stood and applauded. He walked up to the podium and adjusted the microphone.

"Hello Everyone! I am so glad to be here. I agree with Mrs. Smith when she says we have to know our enemy. If you know them, then you can properly plan to take them down. I was never bullied, I was the bully. I didn't like myself and most bullies don't. Most bullies are not as bold as they appear and they are looking for approval. They want to be liked. They want to belong, but their fear has been masked by mean words, fighting and other hateful things.

Before we can discuss why people bully, we need to have a clear understanding of what bullying is. Some consider bullying to be purposeful attempts to control another person through verbal abuse - which can be in tone of voice or in content such as teasing or threats - exclusion, or physical bullying or violence, which the victim does not want.

Now to answer the question, why do people bully? There is no one particular reason and there is no way we can know them all. But here are some of the most popular reasons, some of which I was guilty of as a child." The projector screen lowered and he started his presentation.

1. The fact that the bully gets more attention for negative behaviors than for positive ones.
2. The bully wants power. They need to feel stronger than anyone else. Which by mere essence of being a bully they are the weakest.

3. The bully doesn't have a warm loving family environment at home.
4. The bully has been bullied before. So sometimes they too become a bully.

He walked back to the podium. As I stated before these are not the only reasons, but it does give us insight on how we can start our battle against bullying. I was a child when I did it and I regret it. I am not even sure of the effect it had on the kids that I bullied. However, it affected me enough to join forces with Mrs. Smith and fight this beast!" Everyone applauded. Mrs. Smith returned to the podium.

"Now we that have a few of our enemy's secrets let's see what statistics say about bullying. Then I will share my plan to stop the epidemic that is happening around the United States of America." She walks to the screen.

"Here are a few examples of what bullying looks like. Hitting, slapping, elbowing, shouldering (slamming someone with your shoulder), Shoving in a hurtful or embarrassing way; Kicking; Taking, stealing, damaging or defacing belongings or other property; Restraining; Pinching; Flushing someone's head in the toilet; Cramming someone into his or her locker; Attacking with spit wads or food and the list can go on."

While raising her hand Mrs. Smith asked, "How many of us have experienced any of these?" The majority of the people in the audience. "Yes, most of us in here have. And this is not all. They have cyber bullying through social media such as cell phones, Facebook, Instagram, Kik and even Twitter. We see it in the news every day. Children are being bullied but adults are as well. People commit suicide or even kill their bullies to escape the pain of it.

Here is a side note to our students. You too can help each other in bullying situations. Don't be a bystander. Tell a trusted adult, be a friend to someone being bullied. Help them get away. Be a good example and don't encourage the bully by laughing or instigating. Is that possible?" Sannetta asked shaking her head. The children in the audience answered yes. "I can't hear you." She said. "Can we do this?"

"YES!" The children yelled in unison.

"Awesome!!!! So now you may say, 'Okay now that we know about the bullies and what bullying is, what is our solution?' I am glad you asked." The audience laughed.

"We have started with faculty and staff creating a safe haven for the students to be able to report bullying 'secretly' and safely without having to be afraid of being exposed to the bully. Secondly, the group that is selected from the faculty and staff will choose a group of dependable students to form a peer group to support the victims. They will have forms and sheets that will be kept confidential. On these forms will be the names of the bullies, what they did, and who they did it to. These sheets will be given to the team of adults that will follow through with the principal and properly punish and deal with the bullies. The key to this is to make sure that the bullies are dealt with and that the students that are bullied are protected. We want to also make sure that steps are taken to prevent any further bullying.

At least we can make it hard for anyone to feel comfortable bullying anyone. Bullies will still be bullies, but if enough of us unite, we can stop this monster from breathing. It doesn't stop here with the faculty, staff and peer group. We need each parent to unite with other parents and help the faculty and staff with the follow through. For instance, if your child is being bullied, report it and don't just tell the kids to fight back. I know that is what we were told. If your child is the bully, don't try to defend him/her, show them their wrong and make sure they have some sort of punishment. I know we want to defend our children, but when they are wrong, we do them and everyone else a disservice by taking up for them. We also want to be able to offer the bully counseling to see if they can pinpoint where the root of the issue lies.

Parents let's encourage our kids to tell us and follow up with both teams - the peer and adult advocate group. We need to talk to them; ask questions. We can NOT do this on our own. It is going to take EVERYONE-ALL OF US coming together as one united to start a revolution and slay this giant!" The audience applauded. "As I have said and will continue to say, these are not the only solutions and people will still be people. We can't stop everyone, but we will stop everyone that we encounter. Say it with me: We can't stop every bully, but we will stop every bully that we encounter!!!!!

"Look at what some statistics say about bullying: 40 percent of bullied students in elementary and 60 percent of bullied students in middle school report that teachers intervene in bullying incidents "once in a while" or "almost never".

Twenty-five percent of teachers see nothing wrong with bullying or put-downs and consequently intervene in only 4 percent of bullying incidents. Researchers have found that adults are often unaware of bullying problems.

In an initial survey of students in fourteen Massachusetts schools, over

30 percent believed that adults did little or nothing to help with bullying.

Almost 25 percent of the more than twenty-three hundred girls surveyed felt that they did not know three adults they could go to for support if they were bullied .

Students often feel that adult intervention is infrequent and unhelpful, and fear that telling adults will only bring more harassment from bullies.

Can we all agree that we must do better?" The audience nodded in agreement others applauded.

Finally, though I am not an advocate for fighting, there will be times when we can't be there to protect our children. They may be backed against the wall. I do suggest offering self-defense classes, not just for the children but adults too. In self-defense classes they teach that this is a last resort. This is not to be the first option, but if there is no way out, you have the right to defend yourself. The results that we want to see will not happen overnight, but if we are consistent and persistent we will see a big difference. We have brochures and pamphlets with all of the information that have we discussed today. Also Mr. Fredrickson, myself and our team will stay around after this session to answer any questions that you may have. We will spread the word and travel around the country showing people how we can fight against bullying! Thank you!" She said exiting the platform with a standing ovation to greet her.

Everyone was charged and ready to join forces with Sannetta Smith and her affiliates.

Let's Chat

These questions may be discussed with your parents, teachers and/or classmates.

1. Do you think it would help if all school had a Rally for bullying? If so, why?

____

____

____

____

2. What were some of the pointers that Sannetta Smith gave to the victims of bullying?

____

____

____

____

3. Why do you think bullies bully?

____

____

____

____

4. Do you think there is help for the bully?

____

____

____

____

5. Do you think the steps that were given in the rally could possibly help stop bullying?

____

____

____

____

Chapter Seven

"What Happened To Them?"

In the story with Laci and Traci it ended on a good note. Traci had unresolved issues and jealousy toward Laci. One would think that the roles would be reversed, but they weren't. Because of Laci's sickness as a child, she got most of the attention. In her mind, Laci was better than her and more loved. She was wrong about how she felt, but being mean and hateful to her sister made her feel like she was valuable. Laci didn't commit suicide and they both were able to reconcile and get professional counseling.

Minyom and Aubrey's story didn't end with reconciliation. In fact, they both were suspended again and never spoke to each other again. They were not able to trace the origins of the pictures or videos, but as Principal Johnson said, eventually the rumors and pictures died down. They have both gone on to college and Omar didn't end up with either of them.

Logan's story had a good ending as well. The jailing incident didn't affect his scholarships to the Ivey League schools that wanted him nor did it taint his reputation and ability to play ball. It did go on both his and Blake's record. Though Blake didn't stop his mean ways, he did stop picking on Logan who ended up dating Armani, his sister.

Unfortunately, Chance and Dakota's story did not end with a fairytale ending. The bullet from the gun hit Dakota and she later died from the shot. Both families were shattered and Chance was heartbroken for a long time. He didn't graduate from a charter school. He was homeschooled throughout the rest of his school years. He even enlisted in the military after graduating. The verdict was still out on him being gay. He says that he likes girls and he is sticking to it. By being homeschooled he didn't have to endure the teasing and he was able to feel safe in his own environment. Jaylin and his crew got their act together too. After the death of Dakota, they didn't pick on anyone else for a long time.

All of these stories were fictional, but we can relate with each of them. Either we know a bully, know someone who has been bullied, were a bully or have been bullied ourselves. Whichever is the case, there is hope and help. Every story won't end like the stories we have read, but we can make sure that we do what we can to help all victims of bullying have a good end to their story. Tell an adult, tell a teacher, tell someone so that they can help to protect and defend victims while destroying the monster we call bullying.

One final thought to consider: Why do bullies bully? A common reason that a kid is a bully is because he/she lacks attention from a parent at home and lashes out at others for attention. Older siblings can also be the cause of the problem. If they've been bullied, they are more apt to bully a younger sibling to feel more secure or empower themselves.

Some kids are just more aggressive, dominating and impulsive by nature. It doesn't always mean that they are bullies. Bullies dominate, blame and use others. They lack empathy and foresight and have contempt for the weak. They see weaker kids as their target and don't accept the consequences of their actions. They crave power and attention.

- Bullied bullies get relief from feeling helpless and overpower others
- Social bullies have poor self-esteem and manipulate others through gossip and being mean
- Detached bullies plan their attacks and always likeable to everyone but their victims
- Hyperactive bullies don't understand how to socialize and acts inappropriately and sometimes physically.
- Most bullies don't understand how wrong their behavior is and how it makes the person being bullied feel.

No matter what kind of bully someone is, they have not learned kindness, compassion and respect. Bullies don't need a reason to hurt others. Whatever the reason, bullying is not cool. It's mean!

Write a short paragraph summarizing you thoughts on bullying, how this book has helped you and how this book can help others.

____

AFFIRMATION

(Say this aloud in the mirror each day.)

I am special. I am strong. I am smart.

I will not be bullied and I will not become a bully.

I love myself and I will treat others the way that I want to be treated.

I see clearly and I recognize that it is not right to bully another. I will do all that I can to report bullying to my parents, teachers and Peer group leaders.

I am not afraid. I am not alone. I am courageous. I am bold. I am somebody great.

My words will heal and not hurt. My actions will help and not hinder. My thoughts are positive and I will make a difference in my life and in the life of all that I come in contact with. This is my pledge.

A much needed resource for families, schools, churches and communities that explores effective solutions to the bullying epidemic. ~ Demetria C.

When I read this book I could relate to the stories. It made me think on previous situations that I could've done better with not bullying.. ~ Jenae S. (Student)

I think the book was amazing. All the situations that went down were realistic. I've seen these type of situations go down inside of my school. I think that if teens read this it could change a lot in the way they act and react. ~ Marissa D. (Student)

I liked how it was very relatable because things like this happen every day in my school. I'm glad that Mrs. Netta is showing teens that these things are wrong. Thank you for bringing this issue to light because it is often ignored ~ Lela M. (Student)

I loved the book and the affirmations at the end. I will introduce this to my Sunday School class! This book shows how hard it is for kids sometime. I hope that it gets in all the schools so they can fight against being bullied and the bullies themselves get the help they need. ~ Phyllis M. (Parent)

This book has to be in schools because, as an adult, through this book I was introduced to methods of bullying which I classified as simple "sibling rivalry". After reading this book I kept asking myself "Is this going on in my own house?" I found myself hugging my 22 and 18 year old and questioning my 7 year old about her state of mind. It makes me what to do better as a parent and mentor to the children in the community. Because of this book I will never take lightly the comments children say to me! ~ Tamarra J. (Parent)

The book gives real life scenarios that children deal with in the raw form. Children that are getting bullied need to know they're not the only ones getting bullied and that bullying has been around for years.They also need to know that there are people that they can talk to. They don't have to just "deal with it" because they're fat, ugly, gay etc. Bullies need to read it so that they know the damage & destruction they do on other people's lives. It's not at all funny, but very serious & they need to see that. The school administrators need to read it so that they can be more prepared, welcoming & ready to take action when they witness someone being bullied or when that person being bullied comes to them for resolve; they are usually the 1st ones to see it & witness it & they ignore it & sweep it under the rug, which is why students don't come to them. I love the questions at the end of each scenario to make the students & even administrators really have to think about the situation & put themselves in the place of the bully or the student being bullied. It would be beneficial for students & administrators to go through the book together. Those not being bullied may become more sensitive to the issues, the bullied may get that sense of comfort in knowing that their not alone, the bully will see on the front end the hurt they cause because of their insecurities & administrators will realize the "stand" starts with them stepping up. ~ Takeiyah Davis

By the time many of us reach High School we are either the victim of, the witness to or the actual Bully. This book is a tool for dialogue between students, parents and educators. I would certainly recommend this book to Children of all ages. Annetta has once again used fiction to tell a true story. While reading Bully me not Part 2, I was reflecting on my time in Middle and High School when bullying was tolerated but not discussed. Anyone can tell a story but Annetta Swift has stated a conversation that will continue long after the last chapter has been read. ~ Robert B. (Parent)

I thoroughly enjoyed the book! It's right on time for what's been going on in the schools as of late. I think Annetta covered ALL bases with the array of bullying situations. And I love how she conveyed the message that not only do the victims of bullying need help, the bully needs help as well to figure out the root of his/her actions. ~ Darius C.

Being an elementary teacher, I get to see many issues dealt amongst students, some more popular than others, such as bullying. Bully Me Not Part 2 took on an unusual, but not uncommon act of bullying. It deals with sibling bullying as well. This issue occurs often today, but is often overlooked. I enjoyed reading Bully Me Not Part 2 because it gives a new perspective on bullying. This book should be read by parents, teachers, counselors, and students. Just being aware of what could happen amongst children can be eye opening, and that's exactly what this book did-opened my eyes to bullying in a different light! ~ Daniella A. (Educator)

If you enjoyed this book by Annetta Swift, you will certainly enjoy the rest of her library collection. The books are available at ***www.threreadywriter.com . Below are a few of the other books that will charge your soul as this one has.***

...And many, many, more!!!

About the Author

Annetta T. Swift

Annetta T. Swift was born in 1971 in Cleveland, Ohio to Rev. John and Evangelist Gloria Coates. She relocated to Atlanta, Georgia in 1988 and there she finished her high school education graduating from South West Dekalb High School in 1989. Annetta Swift is a phenomenal author interested in giving the readers a refreshing look at writing from a realistic point of view. She is able to share life's experiences using fictional characters taking the reader to places beyond their imagination. Her writings are thought provoking, humorous, and bring hope to her readers.

Annetta's talents go further than book writing, she also acts, writes plays, and serves as one of the leaders of the drama team "Fresh Manna" at her church. Annetta also travels with her comedy team, "Hattie, Essie and Company" where she stars as Essie Mae Banks. This team brings laughter and healing to crowds young and old. Most recently, she has established a drama club at Tussahaw Elementary School in Henry County (GA), "Let's Act Up Drama Club". They have recently performed one of her plays "Bully Me Not", addressing the epidemic of bullying in the schools nationwide.

Annetta presently resides in Hampton, Georgia, with her husband Rodney and daughter Syrinthia.

Resources

- Bullying Statistics http://www.bullyingstatistics.org/content/why-do-people-bully.html
- Bullying Prevention Program http://bullyfree.com/free-resources/facts-about-bullying
- www.stompoutbullying.org
- Picture for endorsement page courtesy of www.ptm.org
- Pines Public Library – Hampton GA
- Olweus, 1993; Charach, Pepler, & Ziegler, 1995.
- Cohn & Canter, 2003
- Mullin-Rindler, 2002
- Craig and Pepler, 1995
- Girl Scout Research Institute, 2003
- Banks 1997; Cohn & Canter, 2003

Affiliations and Advocates

NPower 2Nspire
Self-defense, fitness and Anti-Bullying
Info @nspire2empower.com
Myra Singleton 678.753.4350

Diamonds & Pearls Sisterhood
www.diamondsandpearlsemp.com
Neka Scott 678-389-1309
email:dpgirlsemp@gmail.com

Ms Pam's Precious Angels Family Childcare Center
6750 Maddox Rd
Morrow, Ga 30260
Pam Lewis 678 642-5396

JBA
PO Box 14883
Atlanta, Ga 30324
Tamarra L. Johnson 404 754 9479
Tamarrapr@iamtalentedmanagement.com

Thomas Pinnacle Learning Center
http://thomaspinnaclelearni.wix.com/terrella
thomaspinnaclelearningcenter@gmail.com
Terrella Thomas 678.439.PIN4

Paper Creations And More by Lorianne
https://www.facebook.com/papercreationslorianne
lori.stallworth@live.com
Lori Stallworth 678.764.3681